W9-AUC-179

GREETINGS FROM SOMEWHERE

The Mystery of the Lion's Tail

BY HARPER PARIS • ILLUSTRATED BY MARCOS CALO

LITTLE SIMON

New York   London   Toronto   Sydney   New Delhi

LITTLE SIMON

An imprint of Simon & Schuster Children's Publishing Division • 1230 Avenue of the Americas, New York, New York 10020 • First Little Simon hardcover edition September 2014 • Copyright © 2014 by Simon & Schuster, Inc. All rights reserved, including the right of reproduction in whole or in part in any form. LITTLE SIMON is a registered trademark of Simon & Schuster, Inc., and associated colophon is a trademark of Simon & Schuster, Inc. For information about special discounts for bulk purchases, please contact Simon & Schuster Special Sales at 1-866-506-1949 or business@simonandschuster.com. The Simon & Schuster Speakers Bureau can bring authors to your live event. For more information or to book an event contact the Simon & Schuster Speakers Bureau at 1-866-248-3049 or visit our website at www.simonspeakers.com. Designed by John Daly. The text of this book is set in ITC Stone Informal. Manufactured in the United States of America 0814 FFG 10 9 8 7 6 5 4 3 2 1
Library of Congress Cataloging-in-Publication Data
Paris, Harper. The mystery of the lion's tail / by Harper Paris ; illustrated by Marcos Calo. — First edition. pages cm. — (Greetings from somewhere ; #5) Summary: "Twins Ethan and Ella are in the Maasai Mara in Kenya, and there's another mystery to solve. Where are all the lions? Ethan and Ella spot lots of cool animals, but the one they're most excited about, they can't seem to find"— Provided by publisher. [1. Maasai Mara National Reserve (Kenya)—Fiction. 2. Lions—Fiction. 3. Brothers and sisters—Fiction. 4. Twins—Fiction. 5. Mystery and detective stories. 6. Kenya—Fiction.] I. Calo, Marcos, illustrator. II. Title. PZ7.P21748Myu 2014 [Fic]—dc23 2013041741
ISBN 978-1-4814-1465-4 (hc)
ISBN 978-1-4814-1464-7 (pbk)
ISBN 978-1-4814-1466-1 (eBook)

TABLE OF CONTENTS

Chapter 1   Wake–Up Call   1

Chapter 2   A Message from Home   11

Chapter 3   The Big Five   21

Chapter 4   Operation: Lion   29

Chapter 5   A Suspicious Swish   41

Chapter 6   Special Visitors   53

Chapter 7   Running Out of Time   65

Chapter 8   Searching for Charlie   79

Chapter 9   The Lion Cubs   91

Glossary   106

CHAPTER 1

Wake–Up Call

Squaaaawk!

Ethan Briar woke up to a strange noise and glanced around, confused. Where was he? This wasn't his room. The bed was covered with a gauzy gold canopy, not soccer-ball sheets. He didn't recognize the tree growing in the middle of the room . . . or the lantern by his bed either.

His gaze fell on the window. A giant bird perched on the sill opened its long, thin beak.

Squaaawk!

Ethan let out a yell. He'd never seen such an enormous bird before—at least not up close!

"What's wrong?" Andrew Briar called out from the other bed. He fumbled around for his glasses.

"Dad! There's a pterodactyl in our window!" Ethan exclaimed.

Mr. Briar slipped on his glasses. "Wow, it's big! No wonder you thought it was from the age of the dinosaurs.

3

I'm guessing it might be a hammer-headed stork. Or a sacred ibis. Wait. Let me look."

Mr. Briar reached over to the tall pile of books on his nightstand. "Okay, here we go. *Birds of Africa*."

Africa! Ethan nodded to himself, remembering. They were in a lodge in the Maasai Mara National Reserve,

which was in Kenya. They had arrived last night with Ethan's twin sister, Ella, and his mom, Josephine.

The Maasai Mara was the latest stop on their trip around the world. Mrs. Briar was a travel writer for the *Brookeston Times*, which was their newspaper back home. Her job was

to write articles about different interesting places like Venice, Italy; Paris,
France; and Beijing, China. This week,
she was planning to write about the
Maasai Mara, which was home to
tons of wild animals, such as giraffes,
zebras, gazelles, lions, and more!

The fun part was that Ethan and
Ella would get to tag along to observe

the animals. The *not*-fun part was
that they would have to return to the
lodge with their dad every afternoon
for their homeschooling lessons.

"I believe our visitor might be a
purple heron!" Mr. Briar said, flipping
through his book. "Apparently they
are very good hunters. Maybe this
one is looking for its breakfast."

Ethan eyed the bird nervously. "There's nothing here for you to eat!" he told the bird.

"It says right here that there are approximately five hundred different

kinds of birds in the Maasai Mara. I wonder how many of them we'll see on our safari," Mr. Briar said.

Ethan glanced at the window again. The bird looked at him and then flew away. Outside, the grassy brown savanna seemed to stretch on forever. There were only a few trees. The dawn sky was a mix of pinks and oranges and yellows. Ethan got back into bed.

Just then, there was *another* noise— this time, out in the hallway.

Knock. Knock. Knock.

Then the door burst open.

CHAPTER 2
A Message from Home

"Rise and shine, my friends!"

The Briars' guide, Kafil, stood in the doorway. He wore a khaki shirt, matching shorts, and hiking boots. A pair of binoculars dangled from his neck.

"Well, good morning, Kafil! What adventures do you have in store for us today?" Mr. Briar asked brightly.

"We have many adventures to look forward to, but only if we leave right away," Kafil said, tapping his watch.

"But it's six a.m.! Can't we go back to sleep for a bit?" Ethan complained.

"Not if you want to see the animals. They like to be out and about in the early morning because it is still cool out. Later, when it gets hot, they like to hide in the shade and take their naps," Kafil explained.

Ethan groaned. At this rate, *he* would need a nap later too!

Kafil disappeared down the hall to help Mrs. Briar pack up their things. Mr. Briar got ready and went to join them.

Ethan had just finished getting dressed when Ella skipped into the room. She carried their dad's laptop computer under her arm.

"You are soooo slow. I've been up for a whole hour!" Ella bragged.

"Liar!" Ethan shot back.

"It's true. I got dressed, wrote in my journal, read two chapters of my book, and checked our e-mail."

"And?" Ethan asked.

"And we have a new message from Grandpa Harry!" Ella announced.

Ethan's face lit up. Grandpa Harry lived near their hometown, Brookeston. Before the Briars left on their big trip, they saw him all the time. Now they spoke to him only through e-mails and phone calls. The twins missed him a lot!

Ella put the computer down and opened up Grandpa Harry's message. She and Ethan leaned forward and read it together.

Hello, my dears. *Karibu Maasai Mara!* (That's Swahili for "Welcome to Maasai Mara.")

Did I ever tell you about my first safari in the Mara? Your grandma Lucy and I loved seeing all the animals. But we couldn't find any lions.

One night, we were on our way back to our lodge when our car broke down. We were frightened. Then, another car appeared. The driver was a scientist named Alex Broad. It turned out that Dr. Broad was studying the lions of the Mara.

Dr. Broad helped fix our car. The next day, Dr.

Broad invited us to go to a famous lake. During the long drive, we mentioned how much we wanted to see a lion. Dr. Broad stopped the car, got out, and imitated the cry of a wildebeest. A few minutes later, two lions appeared—a male and a female! Apparently, lions like to eat wildebeests. So we finally got our lion sighting. (And yes, we drove away quickly!)

I hope your safari is as exciting as ours was. And I hope you run across a lion or two (or more)!

Lots of love,

Grandpa Harry

"Now I really want to see a lion!" Ella said eagerly.

"Definitely," Ethan agreed. "But how?"

"Maybe Kafil will have some ideas," Ella suggested.

"I don't want to try Dr. Broad's wildebeest trick," Ethan said.

Ella shook her head. "Neither do I. I don't want to be a lion's dinner—or breakfast!"

The twins shivered.

CHAPTER 3

The Big Five

The Briars enjoyed a quick breakfast of papaya slices, porridge with goat's milk, and *mandazi*, which was a kind of doughnut. Then they headed outside and crowded into Kafil's car.

"I have sunscreen, bug spray, water, and snacks. Did you remember your hats and cameras, kids?" Mrs. Briar asked, spinning around in her seat.

Ella patted her messenger bag. "Yep," she said.

"Hey, how about my comic books?" Ethan piped up.

Ella sighed. "Yes, I remembered your comic books. Next time, bring your *own* bag!"

"You're not going to have time to read, Ethan. There will be too many exciting things to see!" Mr. Briar said.

Kafil started the engine and headed down a narrow dirt road. Dust kicked up as they drove along. It was very dry out . . . and *very* hot.

"The Mara goes on for many, many miles," Kafil told the Briars. "It is home to giraffes, cheetahs, hippos, hyenas, and many other wild animals.

It is also home to the Big Five. The Big Five are the five most popular animals to see: the rhinoceros, the leopard, the Cape buffalo, the African elephant—and, of course, the lion."

The lion! Ella and Ethan grinned at each other.

"Hopefully, we will be able to see all five during the next few days," Kafil went on.

"We *have* to see all five," Ethan insisted.

"Especially the lion!" Ella added.

"If we are lucky, we may also catch part of the Great Migration," Kafil continued.

"What's that?" Mrs. Briar asked.

"Each year, millions of wildebeest, zebra, and gazelles walk in an eighteen-hundred-mile loop between here and the country of Tanzania," Kafil replied.

Ella elbowed Ethan. "Wildebeest!" she whispered, remembering Grandpa Harry's e-mail.

"Eighteen hundred miles? That's a long way to travel!" Mr. Briar remarked.

"Yes. These animals follow the rainy season from place to place. Otherwise, they will not have water to drink or green grass to graze on," Kafil explained.

They soon reached a grove of acacia trees. Ella thought

the trees looked like umbrellas that had turned inside out in the wind.

Just beyond the trees was a small watering hole.

Kafil slammed on the brakes. "Look! Look!" he shouted.

CHAPTER 4

Operation: Lion

Kafil pointed to a huge animal that was drinking at the watering hole.

It was a rhinoceros!

"Wow!" the twins exclaimed.

"This type of rhinoceros is called a black rhinoceros even though it is really more gray than black," Kafil told the Briars. "Our friend there looks to weigh around three thousand pounds."

"Three thousand pounds? That's the weight of a small truck!" Mr. Briar said, surprised.

Kafil chuckled. "Yes, they are quite large. They also like to be alone. However, they have been known to have 'houses.' Houses are certain areas they like to visit often."

"Aww!" Ella smiled.

Mrs. Briar snapped pictures with her camera.

Ella took her notebook out of her messenger bag. Grandpa Harry had given it to her as a special going-away present.

She wrote:

THE BIG FIVE
Rhinoceros
Leopard
Cape buffalo
African elephant
Lion!!!

* * *

Later that morning, they spotted the
second of the Big Five in a thicket of
shrubs: a Cape buffalo! It was dark
brown and had two curly horns that
angled out to the sides. Several small
birds nestled on its back.

"Those birds are called oxpeckers. They eat bugs and other things that live on the buffalo. It's free food for them, and the buffalo get nice and clean. In fact, I once saw an oxpecker picking a buffalo's nose with its beak!"

Kafil said with a wide smile.

"Ewww," Ella remarked.

Ethan laughed.

Kafil added that buffalo were one of the most dangerous animals on the African plains. "Do not worry, though.

This one will leave us alone as long as we leave him alone," he assured the Briars.

Around noon the group returned to the lodge. The sun was high in the sky. The air felt like a thick blanket of heat.

"What a successful outing!" said Mr. Briar as he hopped out of the car.

"We didn't see any lions, though," Ella replied, disappointed.

"Lions are difficult animals to spot. For one thing, they sleep an average of twenty hours a day in caves, dens, and other safe places," Kafil said. "I do hope we see a lion this week. But there is a chance we may not."

Inside the lodge, Ella called Ethan aside.

"We *have* to find a lion," Ella whispered.

"I know. But how?" Ethan asked.

"Well . . . first we should learn as much as we can about them," Ella suggested.

Ethan nodded. "And what about Grandpa Harry's friend Dr. Alex Broad? Do you think he still lives in the Maasai Mara? If we can find *him*, maybe *he'll* be able to find a lion for us—just like he did for Grandpa Harry and Grandma Lucy!"

The twins exchanged high fives. Then Ella reached for her notebook, opened it to a clean page, and wrote:

OPERATION: LION
1. Learn all about lions.
2. Find Grandpa Harry's friend Dr. Alex Broad. He's a lion scientist!

CHAPTER 5

A Suspicious Swish

Just before sunset, the Briars and Kafil went back out on the savanna again. The air was cooler and smelled like flowers. Birds and other creatures twittered and squawked in the trees.

"The animals should be up from their naps and looking for dinner," Kafil explained as he drove.

Ella opened her notebook. "Excuse

me, Kafil? You told us that lions like to sleep a lot. Can you tell us more about them?"

"Yes, of course! First of all, they live in groups called prides. Prides are made up of adults and cubs. The adult

males are the only ones with manes. The darker the mane, the more powerful the lion." Kafil added, "And speaking of powerful . . . a lion's roar can be heard from five miles away!"

"Wow!" Ella wrote all this down.

"Kafil? Do you know a scientist named Dr. Alex Broad?" Ethan asked.

Kafil nodded. "Yes, of course! Everyone knows Dr. Broad. She has been studying the lions of the Mara for many, many years."

"*She?*" Ethan repeated. He and Ella

had thought Dr. Broad was a man!

"Yes. Dr. Alexandra Broad. I have not seen her in a while. She lives in a tent much of the time. She moves from place to place, following the lions," Kafil said.

"Big Five alert!" Mr. Briar shouted. He pointed out the window.

The twins looked. Three leathery gray elephants stood at a riverbank.

One of them lifted its trunk and sprayed the other two with water.

"Awesome!" Ethan exclaimed.

"Are they giving each other baths?" Ella asked.

"Perhaps," Kafil replied. "Or they could be goofing around. Elephants are very playful creatures. They are also very smart."

"I read that some of the noises they make can't even be heard by humans," Mrs. Briar said as she snapped pictures.

"Yes, that is true. Another interesting fact about elephants is that they sleep only about three or four hours every day. They spend most of their time searching for food. They need to eat a lot because they are so huge," Kafil said.

Kafil parked the car so they could get out and enjoy the scenery. The sun was beginning to set, and the sky was the color of flames.

Mrs. Briar took more pictures. Kafil and Mr. Briar discussed the history of the Maasai people. Ethan and Ella sat down on a pile of rocks.

All of a sudden, Ethan saw a small movement in a far-off bush.

It looked like the swish of a long golden tail.

Did it belong to a lion?

CHAPTER 6

Special Visitors

Ethan elbowed his sister and pointed. "Look!" he whispered.

Ella followed her brother's gaze. "So? It's a bush."

"I think I saw a lion hiding there!" Ethan told her.

The twins stared and stared. But there was no lion.

"False alarm," Ella declared.

"But I saw it swish its tail!" Ethan insisted.

"It was probably an optical illusion. That's when you think you see one thing but it's actually something else," Ella explained.

Ethan rolled his eyes. Ella was always trying to teach him things.

"Maybe you saw a branch blowing in the wind," Ella continued, "and you *thought* it was a lion's tail."

Ethan frowned. Was Ella right? He could swear whatever it was had a fuzzy tuft at the end of it.

But before he could say any more, Kafil called everyone to the car. It was time to head back.

* * *

At the lodge, the Briars and Kafil sat outside around a roaring campfire. Other guests completed the circle. Several conversations were going at the same time in different languages. Ella thought she recognized Italian, French, and Chinese among them. Overhead, a million stars twinkled in the sky.

After a while, some visitors

arrived: six men and six women. The twins gazed in wonder at their outfits. Cloths with colorful patterns covered their bodies. Strings of beads dangled from their necks, arms, and ears. Several of the men carried long sticks.

One of them spoke to Kafil in a language Ella didn't recognize.

"These are Maasai people from a nearby village," Kafil

explained after a moment. "They would like to perform a dance for everyone."

"Cool!" Ethan said.

An elderly man began singing. "He is their song leader," Kafil whispered.

"The others in the group will sing back to him now."

The twins listened intently as the Maasai villagers responded to the song leader's call. As the music continued, everyone's words wove together.

Then the villagers began to dance.
They bobbed their heads back and
forth and waved their sticks in the air.

When the performance was over,
everyone clapped. "That was truly
incredible!" Mrs. Briar gushed.

One of the Maasai women pointed
to the twins and said something to
Kafil. "They would like to invite your
family to visit their village tomorrow—
that is, if you are not busy," he told the
Briars.

"We'd love to! I think we've seen enough animals, anyway. I have plenty of photos for my article," Mrs. Briar replied.

Ethan and Ella glanced at each other in alarm. *Seen enough animals?* A trip to the village sounded fun. But they hadn't seen a lion yet!

CHAPTER 7
Running Out of Time

The next day, Kafil drove the Briars to the Maasai village. On the way, Ella pulled out her notebook and wrote:

Before we went to bed last night, we saw a leopard in a tree near our lodge. That means we've seen four of the Big Five.

We still haven't seen a lion, though.

And today is the last day of our safari! Tomorrow, we're leaving to go to a place called Lake Nakaru. Can we find Dr. Alex Broad? Will she help us find a lion? We're running out of time!

Soon the Briars arrived at the village. They passed a row of low brown huts.

"These Maasai homes are made out of sticks that are woven together. The sticks are then plastered with mud, grass, and cow dung," Kafil explained.

"Wait, *cow dung*?" Ethan burst out.

"You mean, cow poop?" he asked.

Kafil laughed. "The Maasai are very smart. This is their way of recycling."

He stopped the car near one of the huts. Some of the villagers from the night before came out and greeted him and the Briars.

A boy and a girl about Ethan and Ella's age hung back in a doorway. The twins waved to them. The boy and girl waved back.

"Habari!" Ella called out.

"What does that mean?" Ethan whispered.

"It means 'hello' in Swahili. Dad taught us this morning at breakfast, remember?" Ella whispered back.

Ethan frowned. He didn't remember at all. He had been too busy making raisin smiley faces in his porridge.

"Hello!" the Maasai boy replied with a shy smile.

"You speak English?" Ella asked him eagerly.

"Yes. We study English at our school," the girl said. "I am Amina. This is my brother, Jomo."

The twins introduced themselves. Then they told Amina and Jomo about their safari and the animals they'd seen so far.

"We really, really want to see a

lion, though," Ethan finished.

"Yes, lions are amazing!" Jomo agreed.

"My favorite is seeing a mother lion with her baby cubs. They rest in caves and dens until the cubs are old enough," Amina said.

"Aww!" Ella cooed. Now she really wanted to see baby cubs, too!

"Do you know Dr. Alex Broad?" Ethan asked Amina and Jomo.

"She's a lion scientist," Ella added.

Jomo nodded. "Yes! Dr. Alex lives in a tent with a lion painted on it. She came into the village a few days ago."

Ella pulled out her notebook and wrote down the description of Dr. Broad's tent. It was a clue!

The Briars and Kafil spent the next
few hours walking around the village and having tea with some of the
families. Before they left, the twins

asked Kafil to take a picture of them with Amina and Jomo. That way they would never forget their new friends!

* * *

Back at the lodge, Ethan organized his photos from the day on the laptop. He especially liked the one of him and Ella with Amina and Jomo. The four kids stood in front of an acacia tree. Behind them was a stretch of land dotted with bushes and rock piles.

Something in the photo caught Ethan's eye. He hit the zoom button to make the image grow bigger. And bigger still.

He leaned forward and squinted.

Could it be?

There was a lion's tail poking out from behind one of the bushes!

CHAPTER 8
Searching for Charlie

"I don't get it. Why do you kids want to go back to the village?" Mr. Briar asked the twins the next morning.

"Yes. We do need to move on. It's a long drive to Lake Nakaru. I want to get photos of the pink flamingos before it gets dark. Thousands of them live there," Mrs. Briar added.

The Briars had checked out of their

lodge and put their suitcases in the back of the car. Kafil was driving them to the famous lake.

"But, Mom! Dad! We really want to see a lion," Ethan insisted.

Ella nodded. "Ethan thinks there might be one living near the village."

"It swished its tail at us. It might be the same lion that swished its tail at us at the river," Ethan explained.

"Wait, *what?*" Mrs. Briar looked alarmed. "A lion swished its tail at you? That sounds incredibly dangerous!"

"It's okay. The lion was far away," Ethan assured his mother.

"Even still. Never underestimate how fast and ferocious a lion can be," Mr. Briar warned.

"We won't," Ella promised. "Can we go look for our lion? *Pleeeease?*"

Mr. and Mrs. Briar exchanged a glance.

"Okay, well . . . as long as you stay by our sides at all times," Mr. Briar said firmly.

Mrs. Briar peered at her watch. "And let's make it quick. Fifteen minutes, okay? Then we have to move on."

Fifteen minutes? That wasn't much time!

When they reached the village, Ethan pointed to the bush from the photo. "Over there!" he told Kafil.

Kafil continued driving past the village. He circled the bush.

But there was no lion.

"Look!" Ella burst out suddenly.

In the distance was a tent. It had a picture of a lion on it!

"That is Dr. Broad's tent!" Ella exclaimed.

"Who?" Mr. Briar asked, confused.

"Just trust us," Ethan said with a grin.

Kafil drove over to the tent and parked. A woman with a long gray ponytail popped her head out. She held a clipboard in one hand and a water bottle in the other.

"Can I help you folks?" she called out in a friendly voice.

"Are you Dr. Broad?" Ethan asked.

"Yup, that's me," Dr. Broad replied, coming out of the tent.

"I'm Ethan. This is my sister, Ella. Our grandfather is Harry Robinson," Ethan said quickly.

"I remember your grandparents! I met them on a safari a long time ago," Dr. Broad said with a smile.

"Oh my! You know my parents? Really?" Mrs. Briar said excitedly.

The twins told Dr. Broad about their
search for a lion.

When they had finished, Dr. Broad
nodded slowly. "You saw a swishy tail?
Twice? I think that's
Charlie," she said.

Charlie?

CHAPTER 9

The Lion Cubs

Dr. Broad got into the car.

"I know where to find Charlie. Head that way," she told Kafil, pointing.

As they drove, they saw some giraffes munching on tree leaves. In the distance, a herd of gazelles pounded across the plain at rocket speed.

"See that fig tree with the claw

marks? Charlie and the others like to use it as a scratching post," Dr. Broad remarked as they passed a thick, gnarly tree.

The others? Ethan thought.

A short while later, the group reached a field of tall pink and brown grass.

"Hey, Charlie! You have visitors!" Dr. Broad called out.

The twins sat straight up in their seats, waiting with anticipation.

"Chaaaarliiieee!" Dr. Broad sang.

The grass stirred. A golden tail swished.

Ethan took a deep breath. This was the big moment. Did the tail belong to a lion? The same lion from before?

A moment later, a magnificent lion with a dark, bushy mane strolled out. His amber eyes scanned their group. His tail swished again.

"Hi, Charlie. Nice to see you! How's the family?" Dr. Broad asked him.

Swish, swish.

Charlie turned and strolled over to a rocky cave. Dr. Broad told Kafil to slowly follow the lion. Kafil parked the car near the mouth of the cave.

Ethan and Ella craned their necks to peer into the cave. Inside was a female lion. And with her were two small cubs!

The twins couldn't believe it. The cubs were so cute!

"The mom is Sunflower. I haven't named the little ones yet. They're about four weeks old," Dr. Broad explained. "Lions are very protective of their cubs, just like human parents are very protective of their children."

Mr. and Mrs. Briar smiled and each put an arm around Ethan and Ella.

One cub nipped the other cub's ear playfully. Sunflower licked them both. Charlie settled in next to his family and closed his eyes.

Dr. Broad gasped. "I *just* came up with the perfect names for the cubs," she announced. "Ethan and Ella!"

The twins beamed.

This was the best day ever!

* * *

When the group returned to Dr. Broad's tent, they found Jomo and Amina waiting there.

"We saw your car!" Jomo said excitedly.

"We wanted to say good-bye before you left," Amina added.

The twins told their friends about seeing the lion family. They showed some photos they had taken too.

"We brought some presents for you," Jomo said. "I drew this," he added, handing Ethan a picture.

Ethan studied the picture. In the center was a lioness with her cubs.

Nearby, a male lion stood guard. Above them, a hawk circled the sky.

"Wow. You're a great artist. Thanks!" Ethan said happily.

"And this is for you," Amina told Ella, handing her a beautiful beaded necklace.

"This is so pretty. Thank you!" Ella pulled the necklace over her head and admired it.

Ethan gave Jomo one of his comic books. Ella gave Amina a jingly bracelet she had made back home. Then the four friends hugged.

"Please come back and visit us again!" Jomo told the twins.

The Briars said good-bye to Jomo, Amina, and Dr. Broad. As they drove away, Ethan and Ella turned around in their seats and waved.

Just then, they passed a bush.

A golden tail swished.

"Charlie's saying good-bye to us too!" Ethan said.

He and Ella laughed.

GLOSSARY

Karibu Maasai Mara = Welcome
to Maasai Mara

Habari = Hello

*All words are in Swahili

"This is the coolest castle I've ever seen!" Ethan Briar exclaimed.

"It's not a castle. It's a *palace*," his twin sister, Ella, corrected him. "It says so right here in Dad's guidebook. 'Taj Mahal' means 'crown of palaces.'"

Ethan shrugged. "Castle, palace, whatever. It's still awesome!"

"An emperor named Shah Jahan built it in memory of his wife back in the sixteen hundreds," their dad, Andy, explained.

"It's become one of the most popular tourist attractions in the world," their mom, Josephine, added.

"Millions of people visit it every year."

"Wow!" Ella stared in awe at the white marble building. It was really beautiful—and really big, too!

The Taj Mahal was the latest stop on the Briar family's trip across India. So far, they'd visited a tea plantation, a desert, and a snow-capped mountain. They'd ridden on a small, old-fashioned train called a "toy train" that chugged up steep hills. They'd seen lots of temples, including one shaped like a giant stone frog. Tomorrow morning, they were flying to the city of Mumbai, which was on the Arabian Sea. The Briars had never been there.

Mrs. Briar was a travel writer for their hometown newspaper, the *Brookeston Times*. Her job was to write articles about interesting places all over the world. The Briars had already been to Venice, Italy; Paris, France; and Beijing, China. Their last adventure before India was a safari in Africa! While Mrs. Briar worked, Mr. Briar homeschooled Ethan and Ella in their second-grade lessons.

Mr. Briar pointed his camera at

the twins. "Let me get a photo of you kids standing on the steps. Wait. How come I can't see anything?"

"You forgot to take off the lens cap, Dad," Ethan told him.

Mr. Briar laughed. "Right! Okay, here we go! Smile!"

Click! Just then, Mrs. Briar's cell phone rang. She answered it. "Hello? Yes, this is Jo Briar."

She spoke to the person on the other end for a few moments. When she hung up, she said, "That was Mr. Deepak Singh. He is a very old friend of Grandpa Harry, and he lives in Mumbai. He invited us to dinner tomorrow night."

"Is he an archaeologist like Grandpa Harry?" Ethan asked.

"No. He's a spice merchant," Mrs. Briar replied.

Ella looked thoughtful. "You mean he sells spices? Like the ones in the grocery store?"

Mrs. Briar smiled. "Not exactly. In India, spices are very special. They are incredibly pure and delicious."

"Deepak is going to call me back later with his address and directions," Mrs. Briar went on. "He had to get off the phone rather suddenly. Apparently, there was some trouble going on at his spice store."

"What kind of trouble?" Ella asked curiously.

"I'm not sure. Maybe we'll find out tomorrow night." Mrs. Briar pulled a notepad out of her pocket. "Let's go walk around the Taj Mahal before it gets too late! I want to jot down some notes for my article."

Ethan nudged Ella as they trailed behind their parents. Ella knew what her brother was thinking. Sometimes "trouble" meant "mystery." And the twins *loved* mysteries!

* * *

The following afternoon, the Briars checked into their hotel in Mumbai. They were tired after their journey but excited to be in the big city.

Ella set her suitcase on the floor of her and Ethan's room and glanced out the window. There was a lush green garden with a row of feathery palm trees. Just beyond were the gentle blue waters of the Arabian Sea. She could make out a row of skyscrapers in the distance.

Ethan plopped down on one of the beds and opened up their dad's laptop.

After a moment he announced: "We got an e-mail from Grandpa Harry!"

Ella sat down next to him. The twins always looked forward to Grandpa Harry's e-mails. He lived near Brookeston, and they hadn't seen him in months.

To: ethanella@eemail.com

From: gpaharry@eemail.com

Subject: Welcome to Mumbai!

Hello, my dears. *Mumba'ī mēm āpakā svāgata hai!* (That means "Welcome to Mumbai" in Hindi!)

Mumbai is made up of seven islands, including one called Old Woman Island. There are islands outside of Mumbai, too, like Elephanta Island. When I went there, I explored its ancient caves and dug up some very old coins.

My friend Deepak owns a spice store in the Kamala Market in Mumbai. His father used to own it. I hope you get a chance to visit the store.

Love,

Grandpa Harry

PS I believe Deepak has a younger brother named Tufan. I'm not sure if he still lives in Mumbai, though.

Ethan reached into his pocket and pulled out his lucky gold coin. Grandpa Harry had given it to him just before the Briars left Brookeston. It had a hawk on one side and a globe on the other.

"I wonder if Grandpa Harry found my coin on Elephanta Island," Ethan murmured.

"Maybe!" Ella got out her purple notebook and opened it to a blank page. The notebook had been *her* going-away present from Grandpa Harry.

Ethan smiled to himself. His sister was always writing down notes about everything.

Ella found a pen and wrote:

Visit Deepak's spice store.
Deepak has a brother named
Tufan.

Ella closed her notebook and gazed out the window. In the beginning, she and Ethan had not been too happy about going on a trip around the world. They hadn't wanted to leave Grandpa Harry or their friends— especially their best friends Hannah and Theo.

The twins still missed everyone. But their trip had been pretty great so far.

In fact, they'd had amazing adventures in every place they'd visited.

Ella wondered what adventures awaited them in Mumbai!

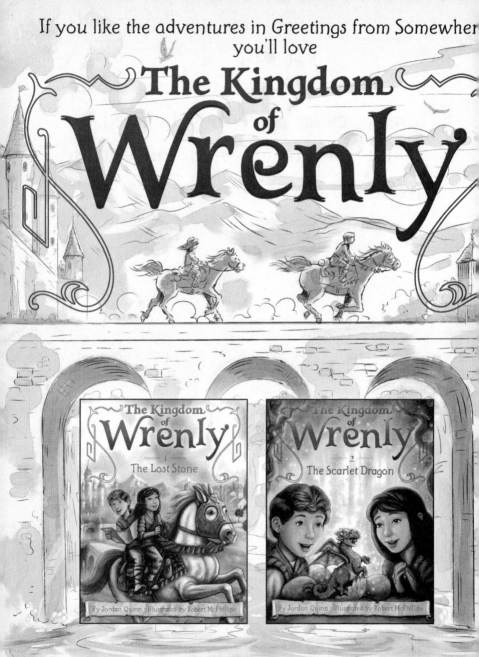